Peter Panda MELTS DOWN!

Artie Bennett • Illustrations by John Nez

BLUE APPLE

*To Mama Panda—and to much put-upon Mama Pandas everywhere—*A.B.

*For everyone who chills out Peter Panda meltdowns—*J.N.

Text copyright © 2014
by Artie Bennett
Illustrations copyright © 2014
by John Nez
All rights reserved/CIP data is available.
Published in the United States 2014 by
Blue Apple Books
515 Valley Street
Maplewood, NJ 07040
www.blueapplebooks.com
First Edition
Printed in China 02/14
ISBN: 978-1-60905-411-3

1 3 5 7 9 10 8 6 4 2

Art direction and design by Elliot Kreloff

Let's meet the Pandas.

Here's Peter. He's three!

And Mama, who calls,

"Climb down from that tree!"

"Settle down, Peter. We've so much to do.

Maybe we'll squeeze in some playground time, too."

"Dropped something, Peter?

There's no need to bawl.

We'll be there in no time—yes, no time at all."

Uh-oh.

Here it comes.

Here comes that frown.

Peter Panda melts dowwwwnnn!

A trip to the market
can be such a treat.

With oodles, caboodles
of great things to eat!

A seat in a shopping cart
adds to the joy.

Mama knows just
what delights her small boy.

Checkout is done and they head to the car.

But then Peter spies a sweet chocolate bar.

Mama stops Peter and firmly says, "NO!"

But Peter won't budge. He refuses to go.

Uh-oh.

Here it comes.

Here comes that frown.

Peter Panda melts dowwwwnnn!

"Don't carry on, Peter. It's such a nice day.

If you simmer down, we'll go somewhere to play."

Peter is quiet on the drive to the park.

There's still time to play before it gets dark.

The jungle gym calls. The swing set does, too!

Oh, where did the time go? My, my, it just flew!

"Let's go now, Peter. We're finished. All done."

But Peter is eager to have some more fun.

Uh-oh.

Here it comes.

Here comes that frown.

Peter Panda melts dowwwwnnn!

"Quiet down, Peter. Behave now, okay?

Let's go to the library. What do you say?"

Brittany Kitten
is reading a book.

Peter slides over.

He just wants a look.

Peter wants that book, too, so he yanks it away.

Mama says, "Peter, that's not how we play."

Peter throws the book down on the floor.

"I'm done and don't wanna read anymore!"

Uh-oh.

Here it comes.

Here comes that frown.

Peter Panda melts dowwwwnnn!

"Stop whining, Peter. Now don't shout or pout.

Here's a nice book that you can check out."

"If you calm down,

I will make you a deal.

For supper, I'll cook up

your favorite meal."

Peter loves pasta, all covered with cheese.

Yet Mama knows pandas must also have peas.

But green-colored food Peter Panda pooh-poohs.

Pure *panda*-monium promptly ensues!

Uh-oh.

Here it comes.

Here comes that frown.

Peter Panda melts dowwwwnnn!

When dinner is done, Mama fills up the tub.

"Peter, come here! I will give you a scrub."

He splashes about with his bath toys afloat—
His ducky, his froggy, his little red boat.

Bathing is fun,

but we aren't done yet.

Shampoo-time always

makes Peter upset.

He doesn't like rinsing or soap in his eye.

"Lean way back, Peter. There's no need to cry!"

Uh-oh.
Here it comes.

Here comes that frown.

Peter Panda melts dowwwwnnn!

"My sweet little panda,
you're clean as can be.
Bathtime is finished.
How about some TV?"

"Beddy-bye, Peter.

A quarter to eight."

"The show's almost over.

Please, please can I wait?"

But Mama holds firm—off goes the screen.

She's put into place a good bedtime routine.

Peter gets mad, and he sends out a scream.

Mama screams back to let off some steam!

Uh-oh.

Here it comes.

Here comes that frown.

MAMA
Panda melts
dowwwwnnn!

TIME OUT, MAMA PANDA.

Mama calms down and puts Peter to bed.

She flicks on his night-light and kisses his head.

Is Peter done melting down for the day?

Is his face scrunching up in that Peter-ish way?

Is that a meltdown? Is that a frown?

Shhhh! No need to worry.

Peter Panda beds dowwwwnnn!